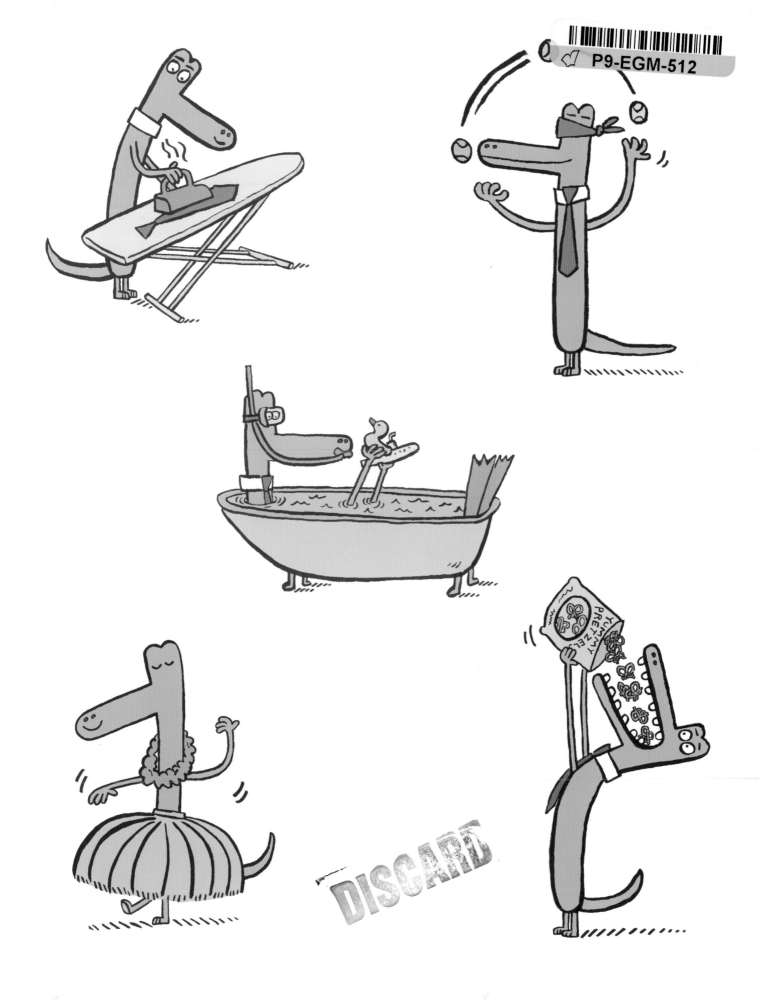

SNAPPSY
THE ALLIGATOR

Did Not Ask
to Be in This
Book!

Words by Julie Falatko

Pictures by Tim Miller

VIKING

Snappsy the alligator wasn't feeling
like himself.
His feet felt draggy.
His skin felt baggy.
His tail wouldn't swish this way and that.
And, worst of all, his big jaw wouldn't SNAP.

So Snappsy went off in search of food.

He walked along the edge of the pond.

He scooted up the tall, tall hill.

He shimmied through the forest.

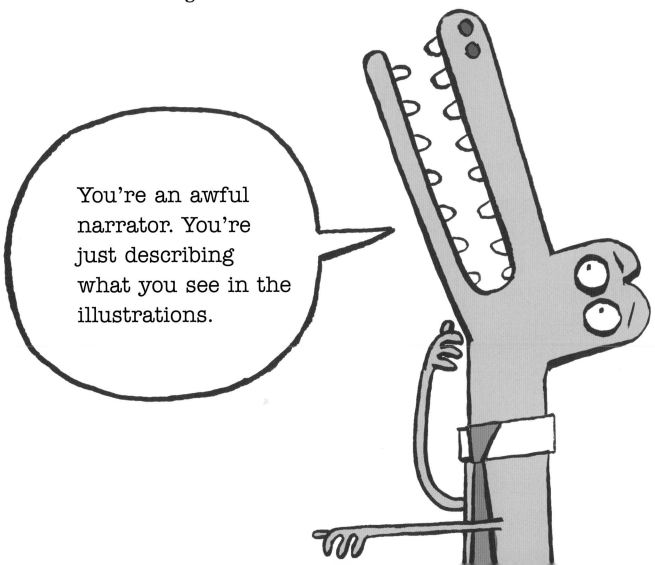

Snappsy, the big, mean alligator, kept looking for food. He liked to eat tiny, defenseless birds and soft, fuzzy bunnies.

He prowled through the forest, looking for victims, when he came to a—

Snappsy looked hungrily at the other shoppers . . .

. . . while loading his cart with pudding, peanut butter, pita bread, and popcorn. Yes, Snappsy the alligator was particularly fond of a certain letter of the alphabet.

Snappsy, the big, mean, hungry alligator, who only liked food that started with the letter P, carried his groceries back through the forest, back down the hill, back around the pond, until he got to a surprisingly lopsided shack.

I'll say.

Snappsy the alligator took his groceries into his splinter-laden shed and slammed the door. Quite hard.

He was inside.

Still inside.

What was he doing in there? Was he making crafty plans? Was he roasting innocent forest creatures that he already had stored in his freezer? Had he fallen asleep?

Well, you have to come out. The story is really boring now.

Snappsy the alligator, trying to better his reputation with the other animals, decided to throw a party.

Snappsy vacuumed the rug. He made goody bags for all his guests. Wait, those aren't goody bags. He's just taking out the garbage. Snappsy should really put out goody bags for his guests. They love those.

Snappsy's party was shaping up to be quite a festive event.

Colorful streamers hung from the ceiling. There were cubes of cheese and a bowl of punch. Some kind of danceable music was playing. Then Snappsy's friends started to arrive.

They were laughing and dancing. They weren't hungry or thirsty.

They looked like they were having a really good time.
Yes, a fine time indeed . . .

All the important guests had finally arrived. And while Snappsy's sharp teeth were still glinting menacingly, he was actually a lovely host.

And we all ate pudding
and did the Chicken Dance.

We were really looking forward to Snappsy throwing parties like this every week.

For Henry, Eli, Zuzu, and Ramona,
who like all food that starts with the letter P.
—J.F.

For Mom & Dad.
Thanks for all that love and support stuff. I think it paid off.
—T.M.

VIKING
Penguin Young Readers Group
An imprint of Penguin Random House LLC
375 Hudson Street
New York, New York 10014

First published in the United States of America by Viking,
an imprint of Penguin Random House LLC, 2016

Text copyright © 2016 by Julie Falatko
Illustrations copyright © 2016 by Tim Miller

LIBRARY OF CONGRESS CATALOGING-IN-PUBLICATION DATA IS AVAILABLE
ISBN: 978-0-451-46945-8

Set in ITC Cheltenham and ITC American Typewriter
Printed in China

1 3 5 7 9 10 8 6 4 2

The pictures in this book were made with brush and ink and
computer hocus-pocus.

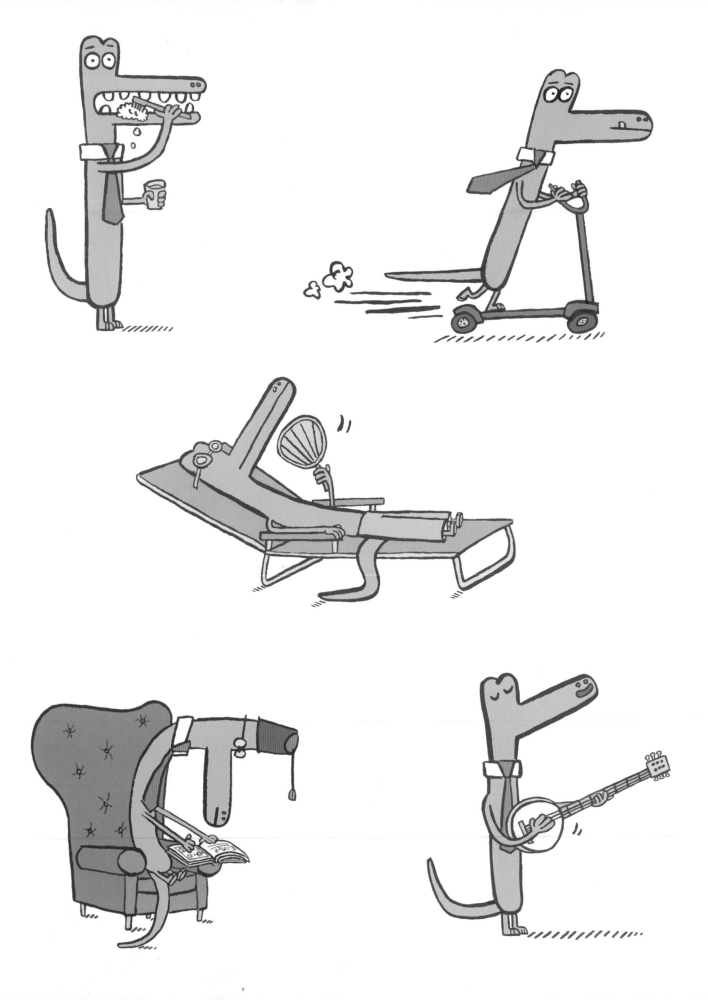